I0783665

KINDLY WOODSMEN

Dale Lazarov & Sebas Martín

KINDLY WOODSMEN

StickyGraphicNovels.com

Printed and distributed by
ComicMix, LLC.,
71 Hauxhurst Ave. Suite B
Weehawken, NJ 07086.
http://www.comicmix.com

Hardcover ISBN: 978-1-939888-59-4

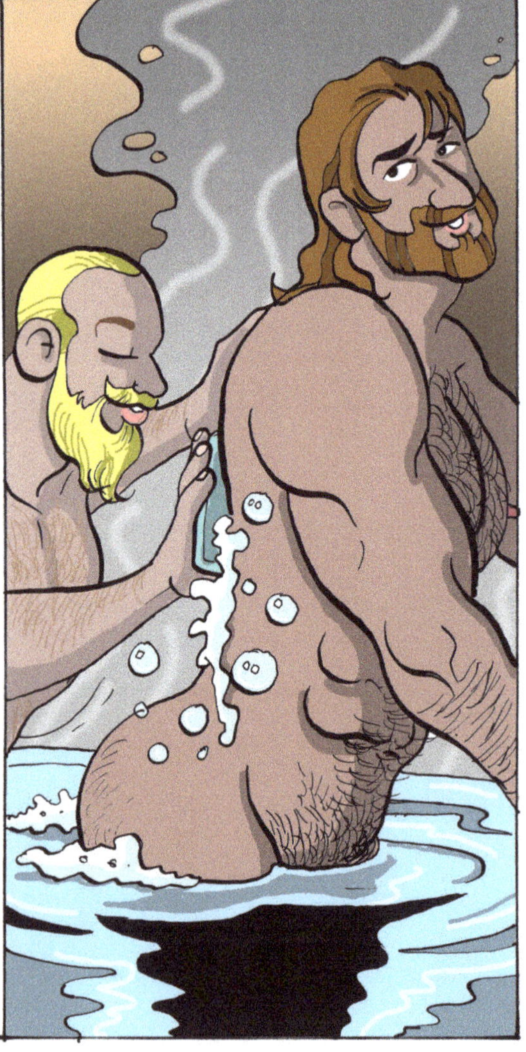

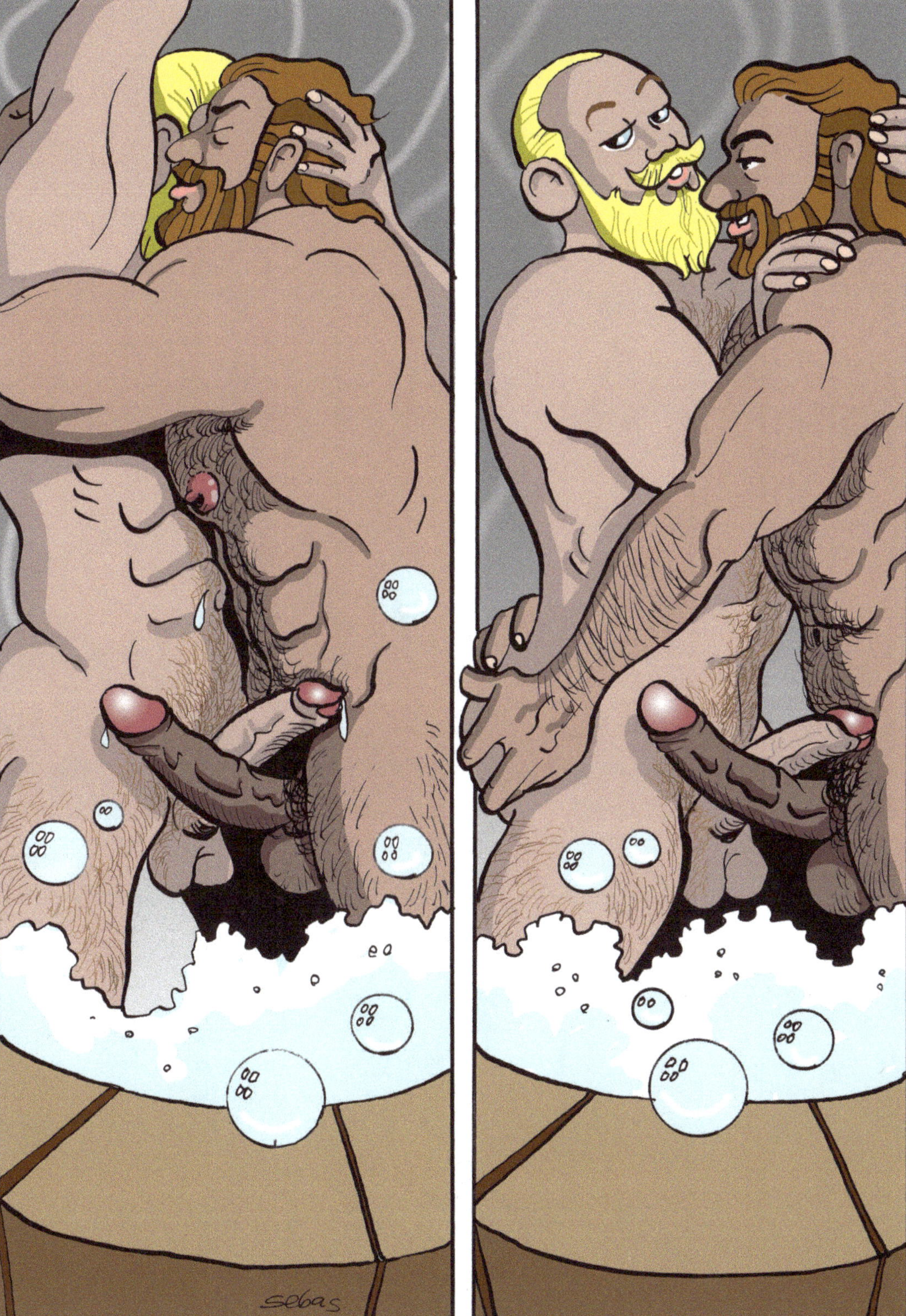

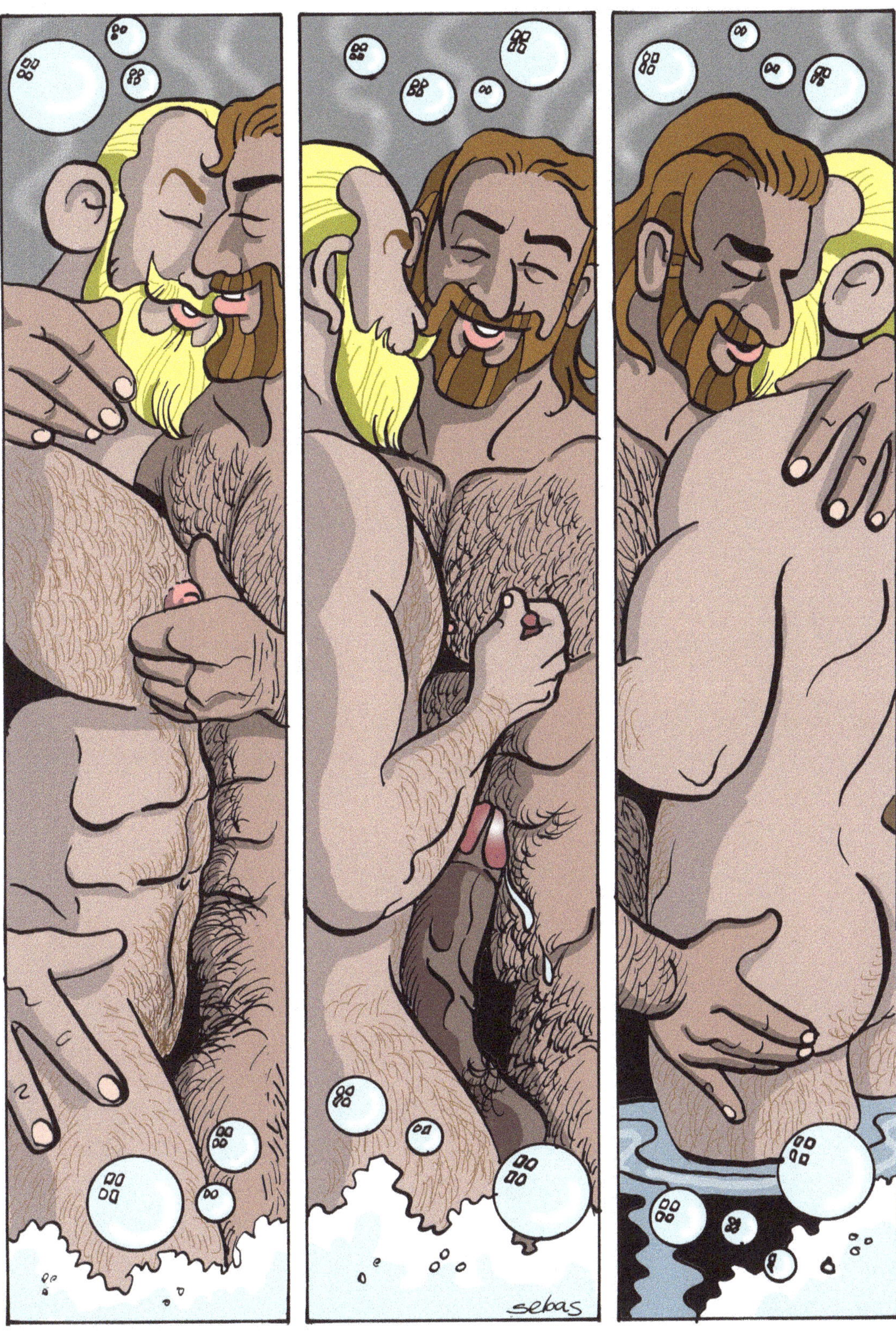

sebas

Sebas

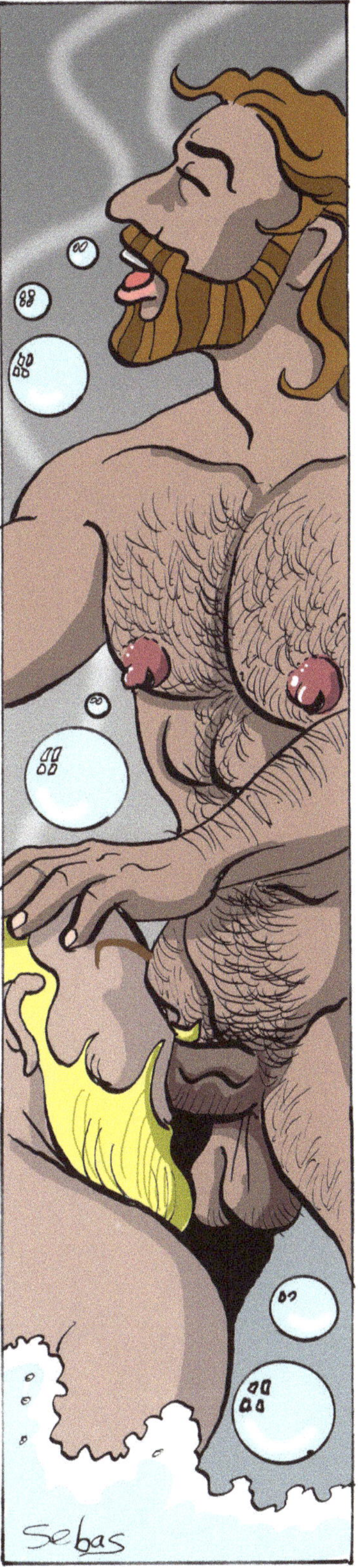

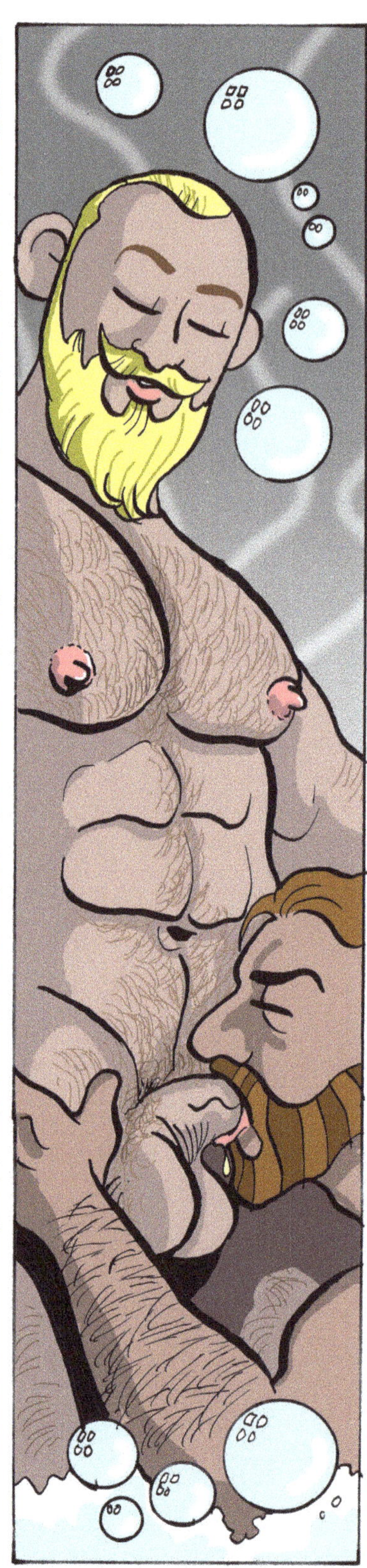
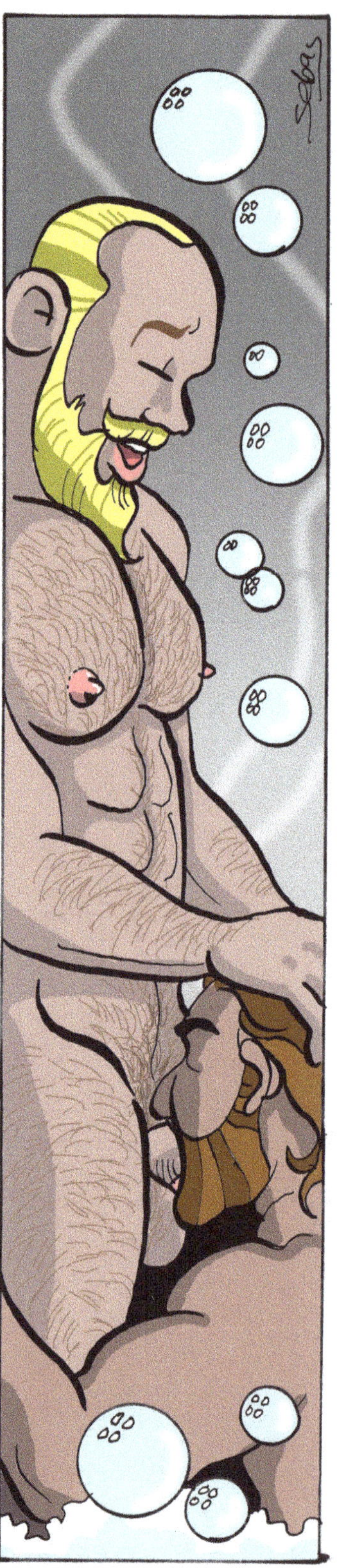

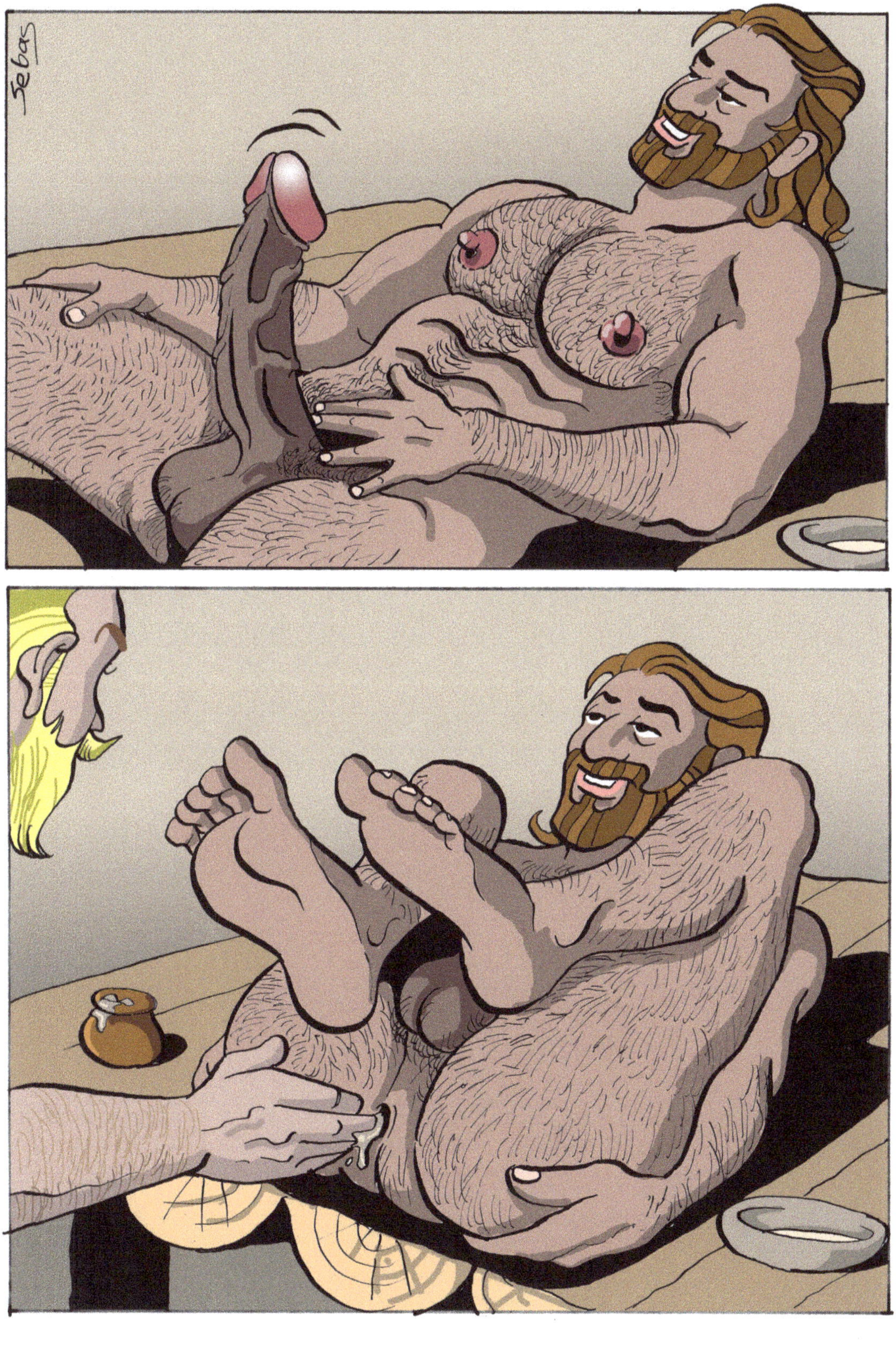

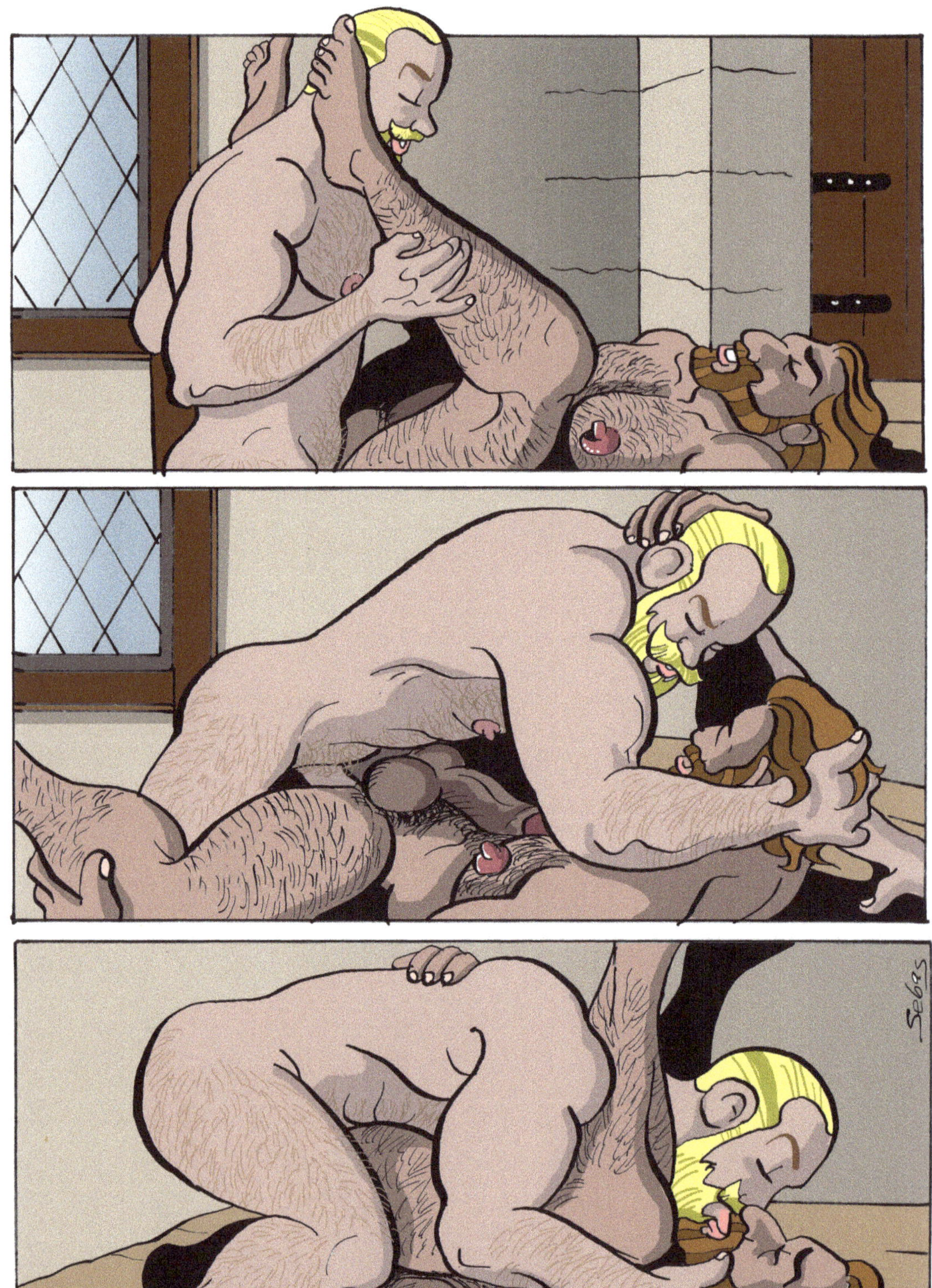

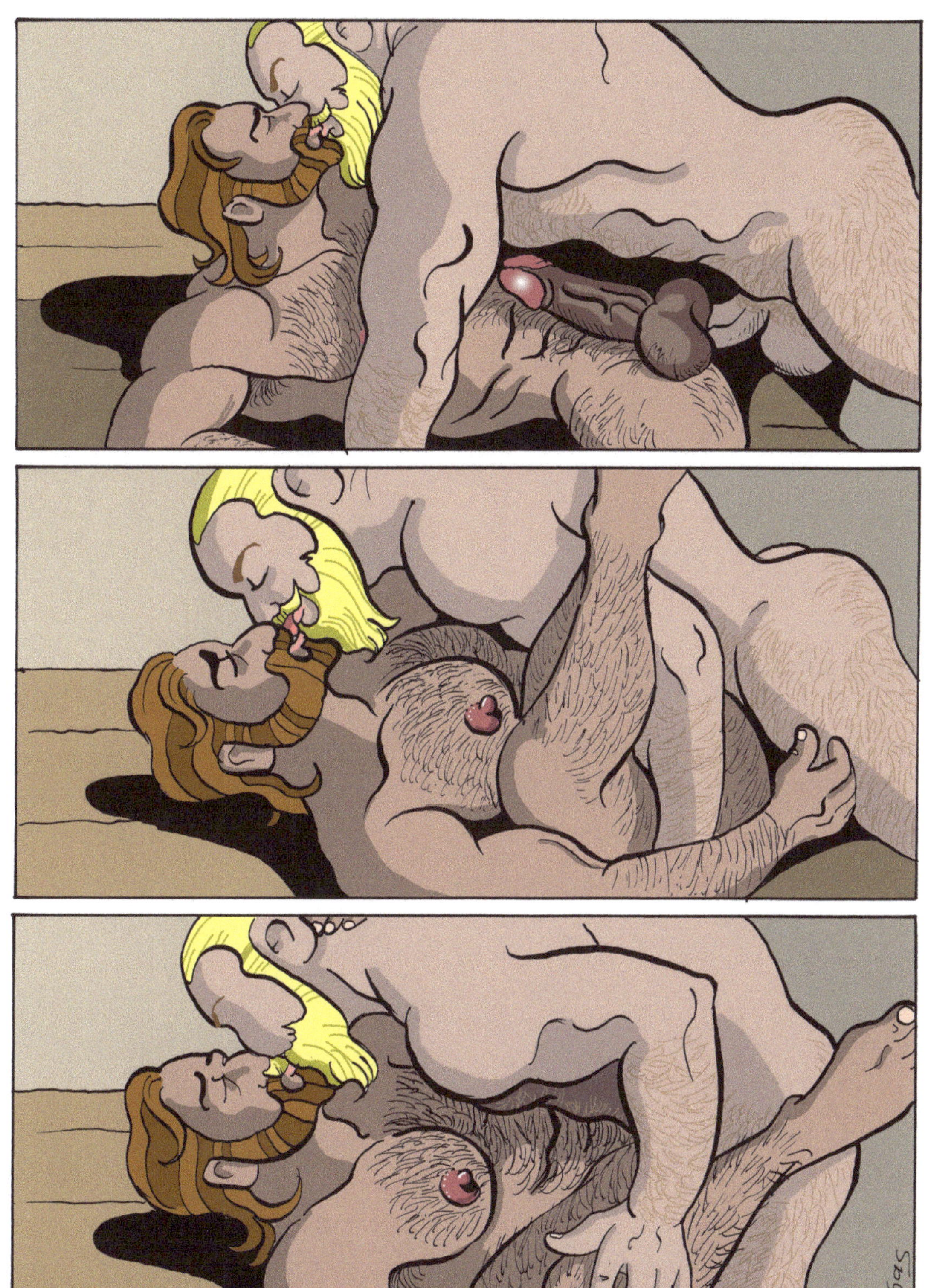

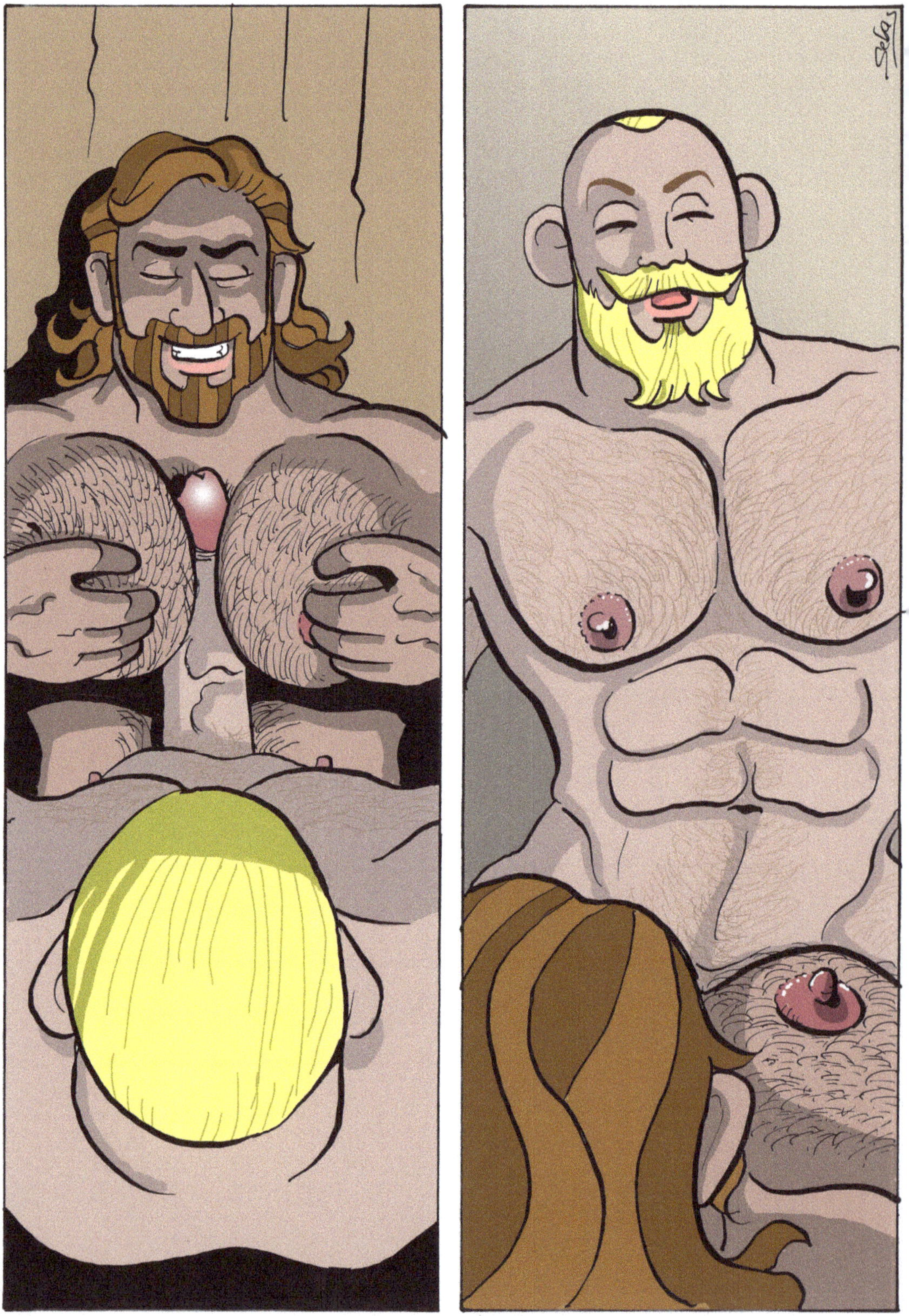

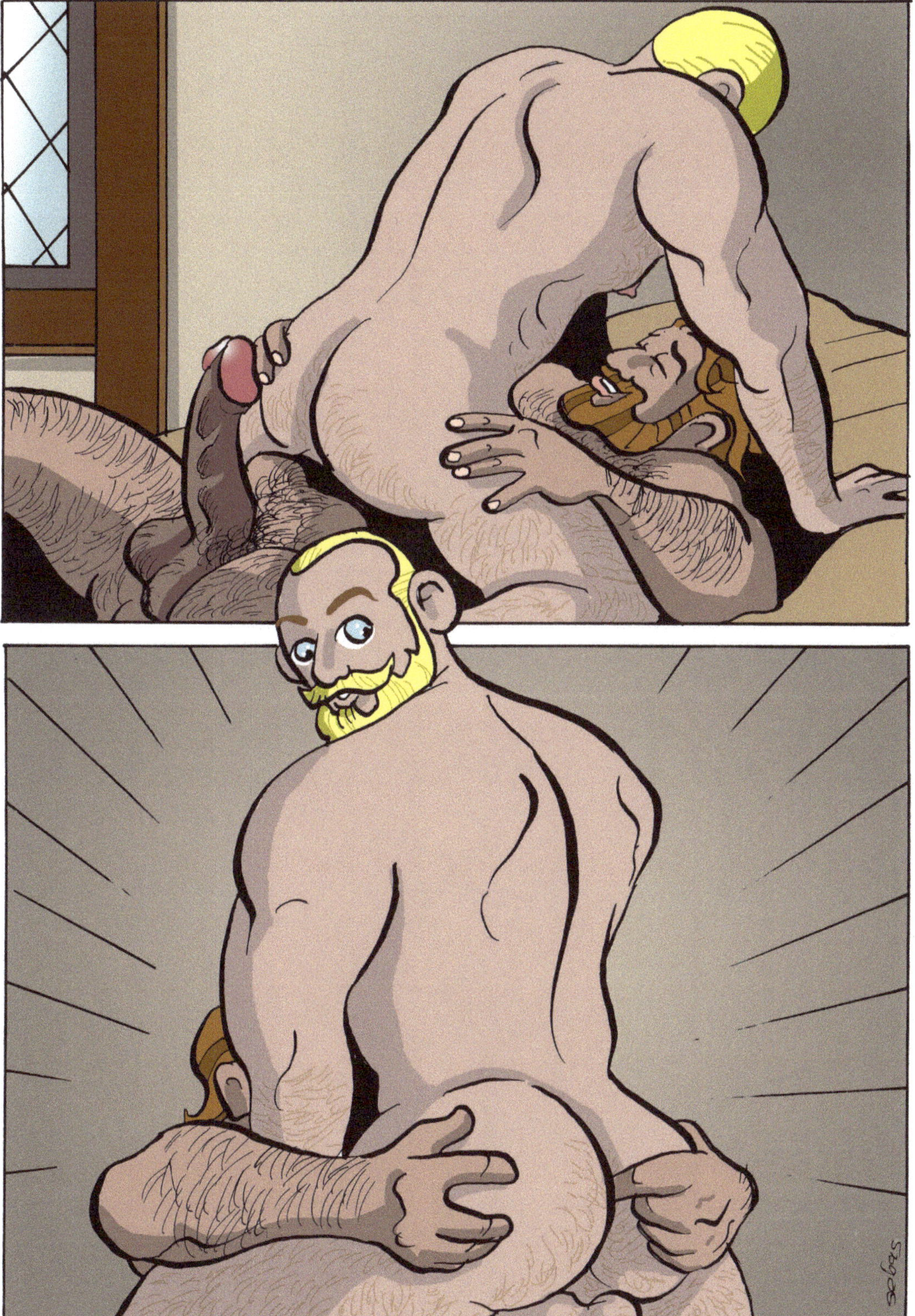

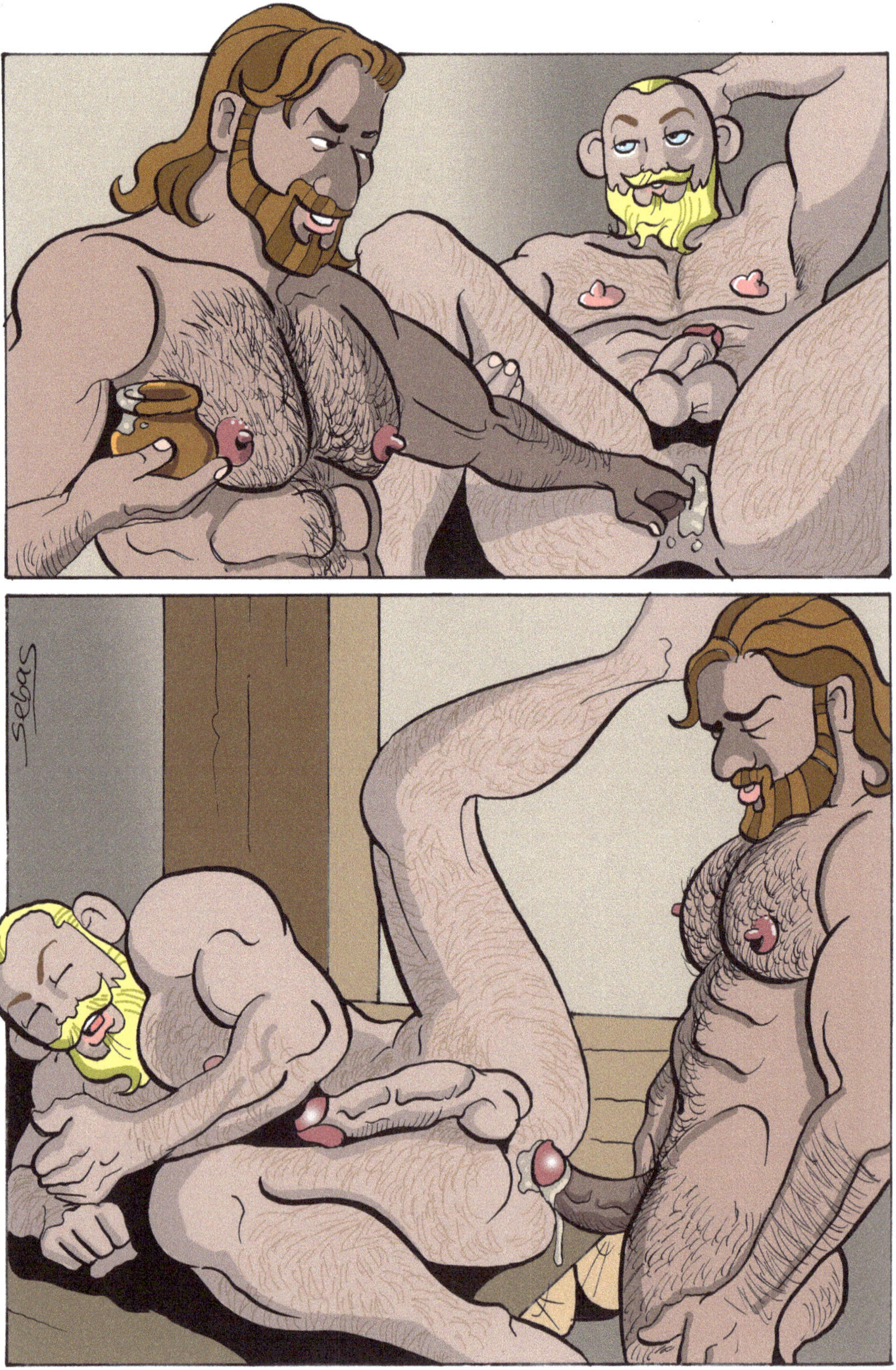

sebas

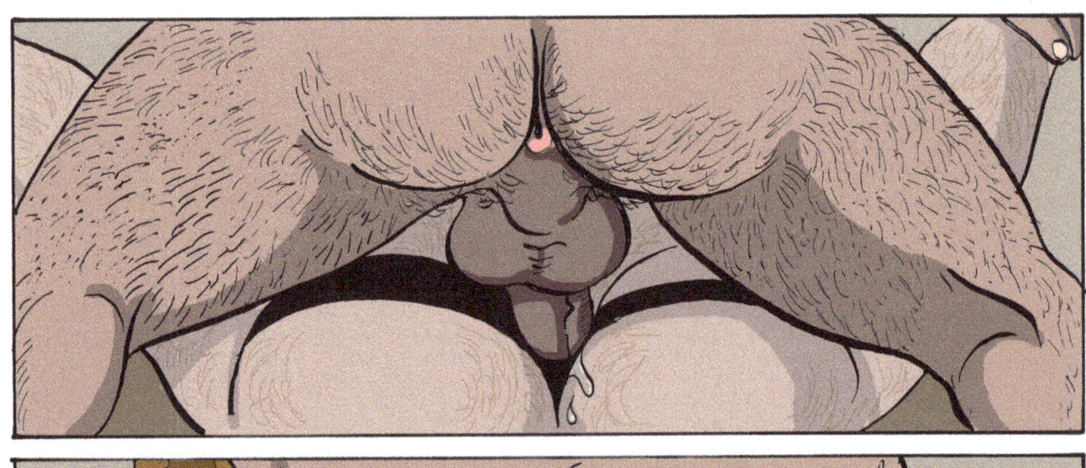

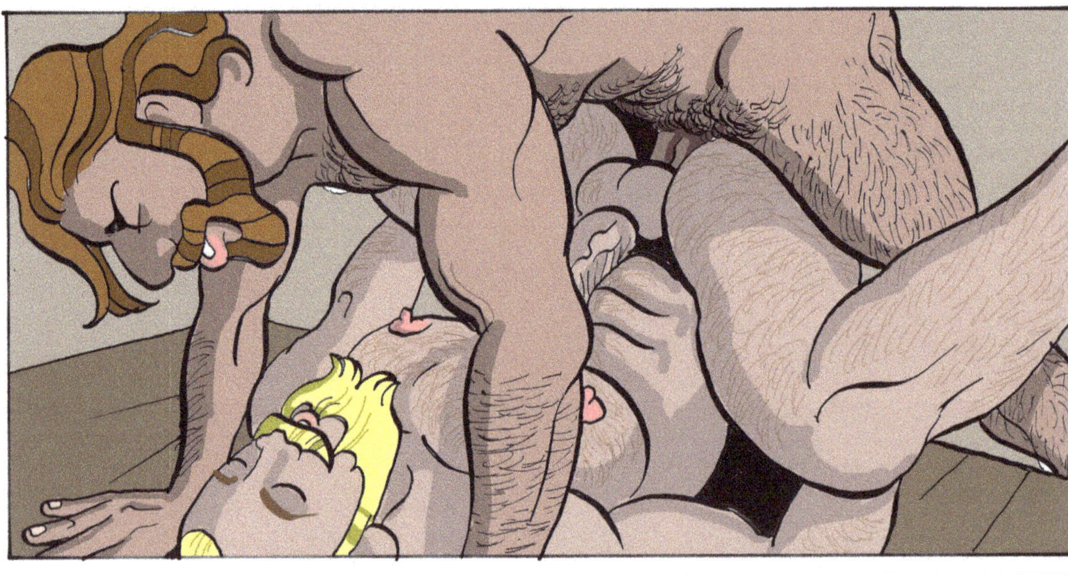

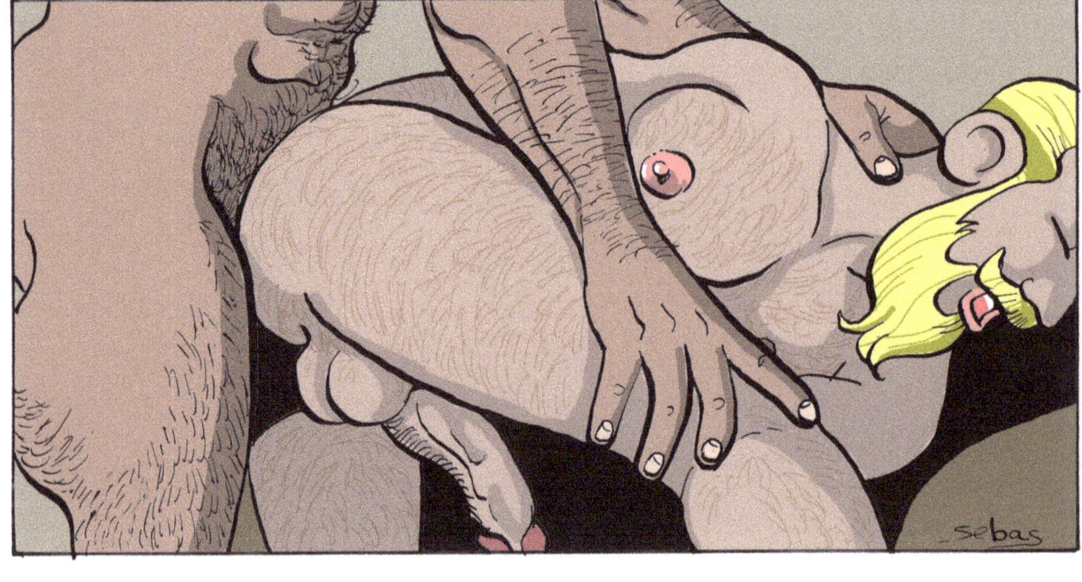
sebas

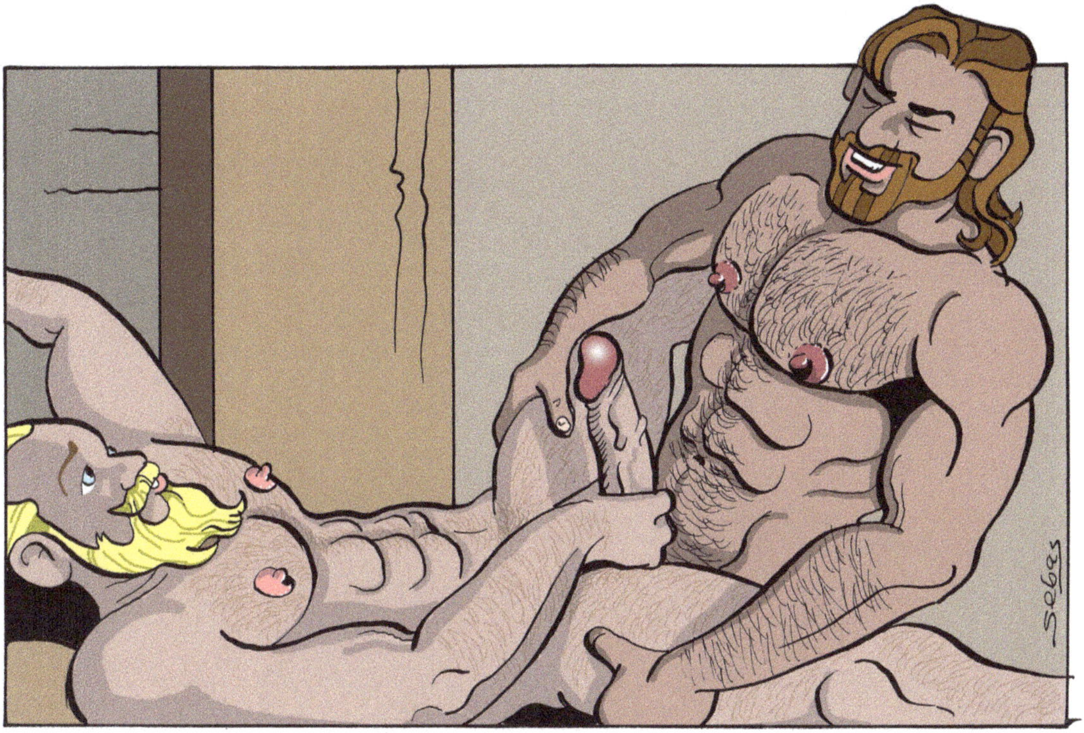

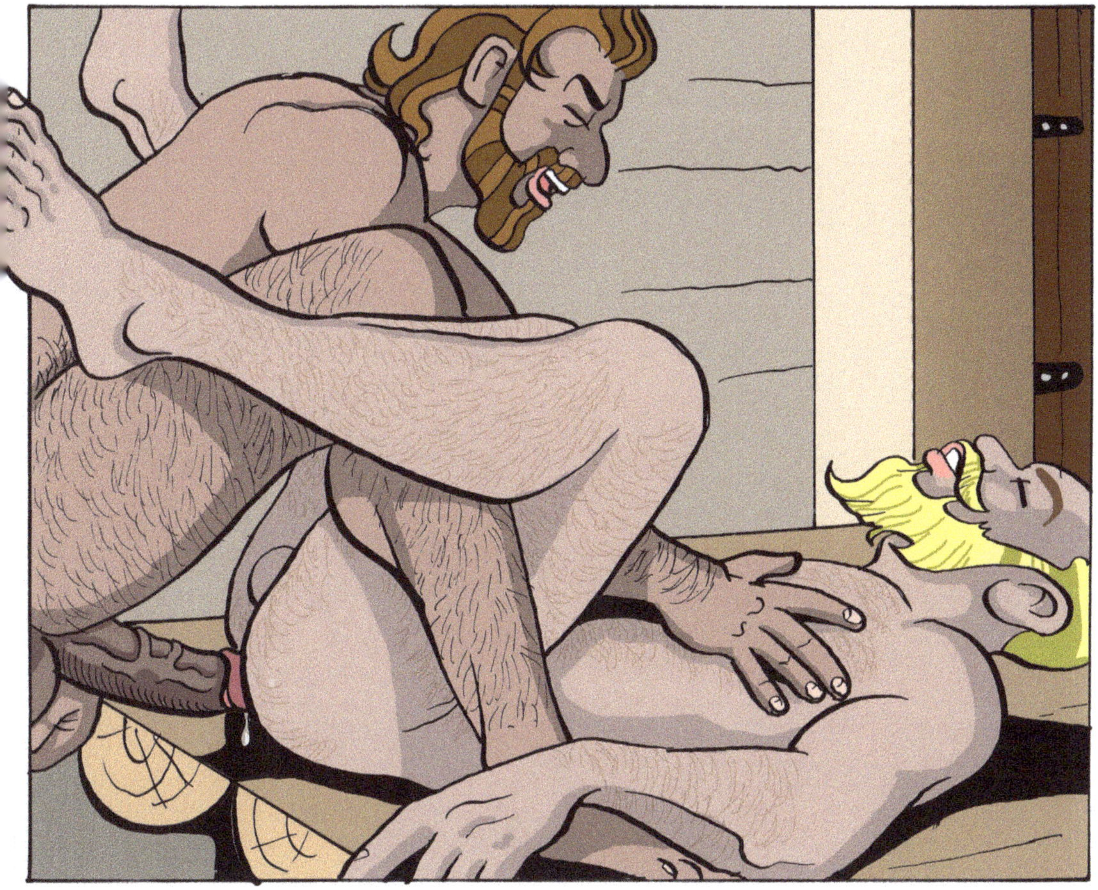

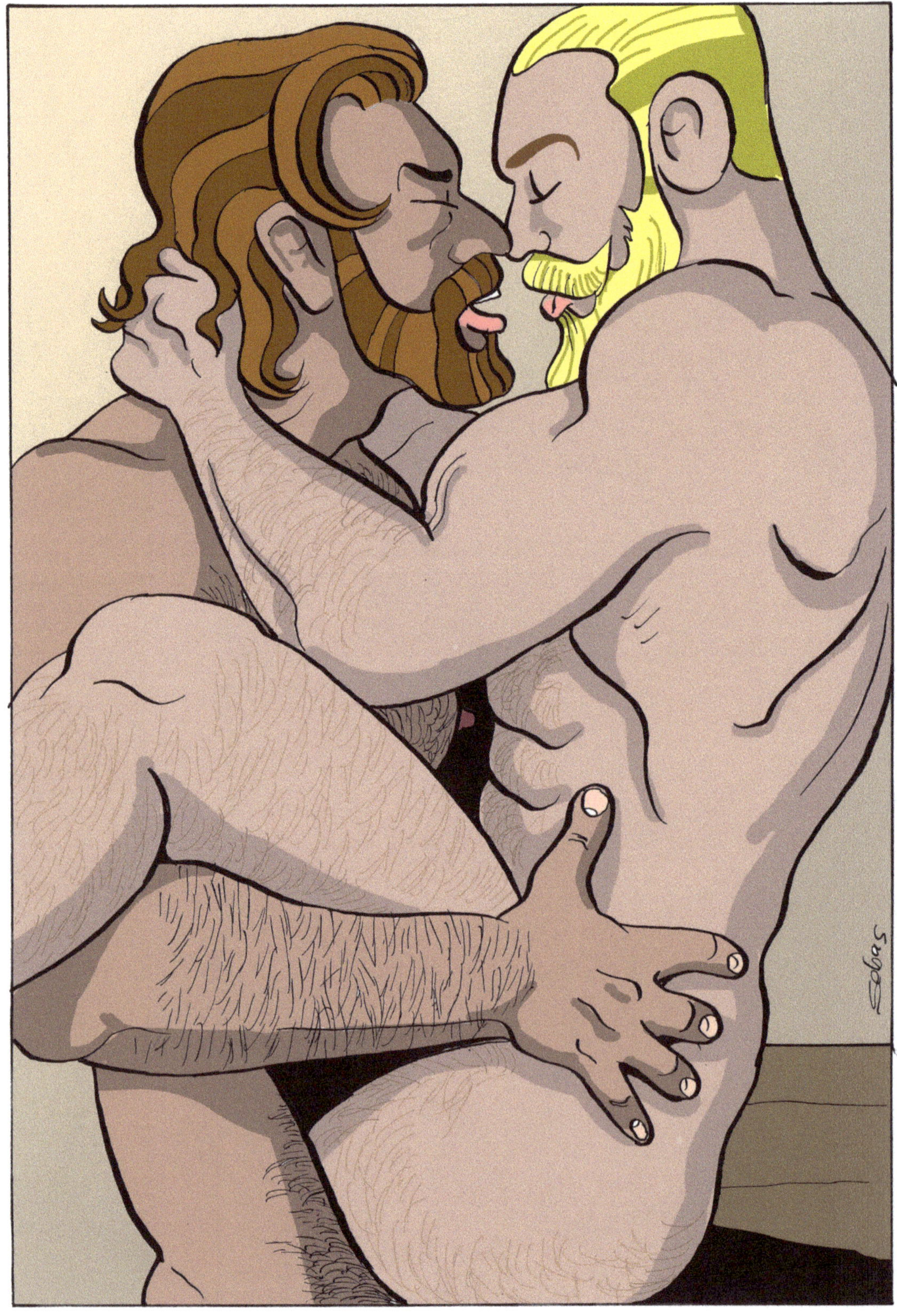

sebas

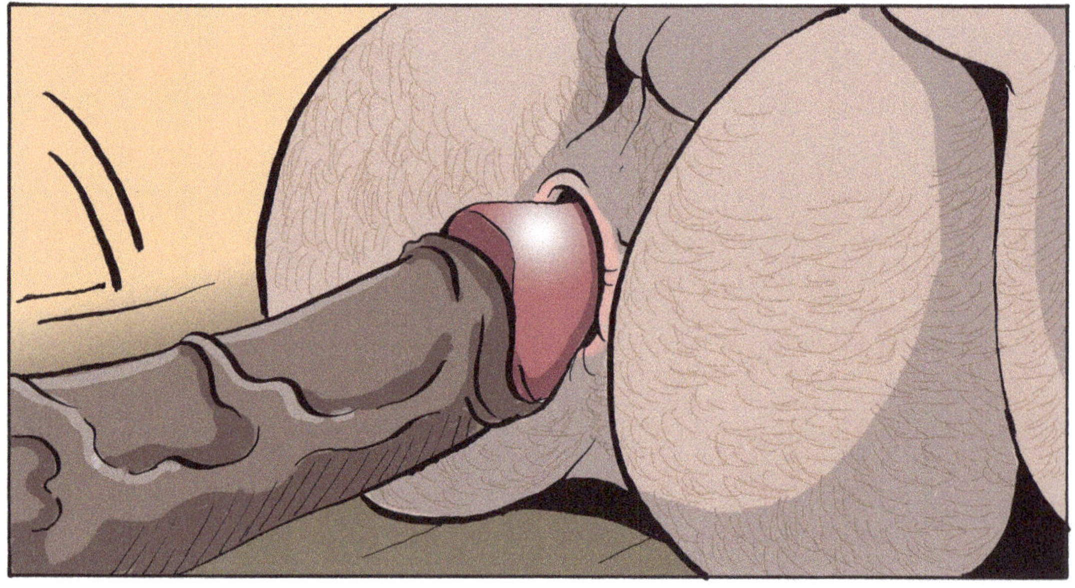

sebas

sebas

About The Authors:

Dale Lazarov is the writer, art director and licensor of Sticky Graphic Novels -- wordless, gay character-based, sex-positive graphic novels for an international audience. Since 2006, he has collaborated on 12 hardcover Sticky Graphic Novels and 39 digital editions with distinctive and evocative gay comics artists from around the globe. He lives in Chicago.

Sebas Martín is a cartoonist from Barcelona who has received the 1999 Casal Lamda Award for comics and the 2000 Serra y Moret Award. He has written and drawn eight graphic novels published by the Spanish alternative comics publisher La Cúpula: *Estoy en ello, Aún estoy en ello, Los chulos pasan pero las hermanas quedan, Yo lo vi primero, Ideas de Bombero, Kedada, No debí enrollarme con una moderna* and *Demasiado Guapo.* He's illustrated the humor comic strips *Arturo, uno de los nuestros* for *Servi G* and *Laia y James en los Eurogames* for the 2008 Eurogames. He has also produced illustrations for many newspapers and magazines such as *El Observador, Nois, Zero, Shangay, GB Magazine, Destinos* and *Toyland.* He's taught at the Escola de Cómic Joso, Escola d'Umanitats del Ateneu Barcelones and the Escola Elisava.